SPACE PIRATE

Sardine vs. the brainwashing machine

SQUARE
FISH

An Imprint of Macmillan

For information, address Square Fish, 175 Fifth Avenue, New York, N.Y. 10010.

Originally published in France in 2001 under the titles *La machine à laver la cervelle* and *Les voleurs de yaourts* by Bayard Editions, Paris.

Library of Congress Cataloging-in-Publication Data

Guibert, Emmanuel.
Sardine in outer space / Emmanuel Guibert and Joann Sfar ; translated by Sasha Watson ;
colorist, Walter Pezzali ; letterer, François Batet.—1st American ed.
p. cm.
Translations of stories originally published separately in French.

ISBN-13: 978-0-312-38445-6 / ISBN-10: 0-312-38445-9

1. Graphic novels. I. Sfar, Joann. II. Title.
PN6747.G85A2 2006
741.5'944—dc22
2005021790

Originally published in the United States by First Second, an imprint of Roaring Brook Press
Design by Danica Novgorodoff

Square Fish logo designed by Filomena Tuosto

First Square Fish Edition: October 2008
10 9 8 7 6 5 4 3 2 1
www.squarefishbooks.com

SPACE PIRATE
Sardine vs. the brainwashing machine
Stories by Emmanuel Guibert
Pictures by Joann Sfar
Color by Walter Pezzali
Translation by Sasha Watson
:01
GAME
GAME
MISS

Contents

Writer: Emmanuel Guibert
Artist: Joann Sfar
The Brainwashing Machine
Today we're going to break into one of Supermuscleman's orphanages and set all your friends free. How do you like that, kids?
Yes!
Yes!
Yes!
Yes!
Yes!
Yes!
Yes!
Yes!
Yes!
Yes!
Yes!
Yes!
Me first!

Please, you be the judge, great Supermuscleman. This is our brainwashing machine.

WONDERFUL! Which button do I press?

First, press the Select key. A child will drop into the machine.
Supermuscle-man, you're a dirty bedpan!
Ew . . . That one was particularly filthy. . . .
I'll press VERY DIRTY!
This Toxiwash® detergent fluid slowly fills the machine. . . .
Krok, you old schmuck!!
Can't we turn off the sound?
Then we rinse the brain and spin it dry. . . .
Add a little brain softener to this one!

There! The child has regained his charming innocence. He is ready to obey.
Who's laughing now, huh?
That'll teach you, you little show-off!
Hack!

I'm very pleased with your work, Professor Hackalack. You'll get a medal for this.
Oh, thank you, great Supermuscleman!
BZZZ
Excuse me, great Supermuscleman. Someone's at the door.
Go ahead! Krok and I are gonna wash another brain.
Yeah!
Click!

BZZZZZ
A medal!
Coming! Coming!

Can I help you?
We're here with the Toxiwash® delivery!

Please be quick, and don't make a mess. The great Supermuscleman is here inspecting the facilities!
No problem! We're pros!
Psshhhh... Hee hee hee!
Hush, Little Louie!

These men are here to refill our Toxiwash® detergent fluid!
Hurry it up!
Hi, folks!

All right, kids, you empty out the rest of the Toxiwash® and I'll mix up the replacement fluid.
OK, Uncle Yellow.

Everything OK?
Glugging away!
Glug
Glug
Glug

Bye now, folks!
All done. They're leaving.
Move it!

QUICK! The second part of the plan!
Fill the water guns with the Toxiwash® from the machine!
And change your costumes!

What's wrong with this thing, Hackalack? I'm pressing the button, but no kids are coming out. . . .
Um . . . There are no more brains left to wash, Supermuscleman!
click! click! click!
click!

There are ALWAYS more brains to wash, Hackalack! Go find one or I'll wash yours instead!
Ri . . . Right away, oh, great Sup . . .
BZZZ

BZZZ
~~My~~ ~~medal~~!
It's that blasted doorbell again!

Can I help you?
I'm Professor SCRIBBLESCRABBLE. I've got a new load of kids for you.

Perfect timing! Supermuscleman happens to be here inspecting the facilities. Follow me. And behave yourselves!
No problem! We always do!
Pfsshhh... Hee hee hee!
Hush, Sardine!

Oh, great Supermuscleman, here's a whole classful of brains to wash!
Very good, Hackalack. You can have your medal after all.
Come on, kids! LINE UP!
Clap! Clap!

Supermuscleman, may I suggest that you wash all of their brains at once!
Which button do I press?
Whistle while you work!
Supermuscleman's a jerk!!
Hackalack . . .
. . . deserves a smack!
They need deep cleaning! Press all the buttons at once!
Can I press, too?
CLICK CLICK CLICK CLICK CLICK CLICK CLICK CLICK CLICK CLICK CLICK CLICK CLICK CLICK CLICK CLICK
Don't worry, guys, drink up. It's not Toxiwash®, it's pink lemonade!

How'd you like that, smart alecks?
Not too big for your britches now, are you?
That took the bite out of them.

You think so?

Guess what's in our water guns, Supermuscleman!
YELLOW SHOULDER! YOU MUTINEER!

Your favorite, Toxiwash®!

Doesn't look like the brainwashing machine is doing anything. . . .

Guys this dumb need triple-washing, Sardine!

THE END!

Writer: Emmanuel Guibert
Artist: Joann Sfar
Merry Christmas, Supermuscleman!
Is that you, Captain Yellow Shoulder? I'm here to drop off the presents. . . .
Sardine! Little Louie! It's Santa Claus!
NOEL EXPRESS

Don't bother waking the kids. Just give 'em this for me.
That's it?
Yup! See you next year!
Wait one minute. . . .
You've got a rocket ship stuffed full of presents and all you're giving me is this little trinket?
You gotta have cash if you want the good ones.
OH, YEAH?!
YEAH!

Later . . .
Wake up, kids! It's Christmas!
We weren't sleeping! We waited up all night!
Snore ...
Where'd you get that costume, Uncle Yellow?
This guy loaned it to me.
Everything in here is for you. Pick whatever you want. And no fighting!
Yay!
First dibs!

Hey, Captain, is this some kind of joke?
WHAT?!
You know who these are for?!
I told you, they're for you!
NO! They're all for Supermuscleman.
They are? Let me see....
Supermuscleman
Supermuscleman
er muscleman
A stink bomb!
Pollution powder!
A do-it-yourself torture rack!
Blimey! What're we gonna do with all this stuff?
Heeheehee! We should deliver it to Supermuscleman ourselves!

Meanwhile, in outer space...
I don't understand, Krok. He should have been here hours ago. Do you think he forgot about me?
Don't worry, Supermuscleman. Here, put on your robe. It's getting chilly.
Do you think he came and we didn't hear him? Maybe he thought no one was home so he left
No, he would've drunk the hot chocolate you left out for him. The cup's still full!
SM
Maybe he just doesn't like me anymore.
Knock! Knock! Knock!
KROK! THAT'S HIM!!
There he is!

WAAAH!
What now?
NO ONE'S THERE!
But, wait! Look!
His cup is empty. He did come!
Then where are my presents?
Your presents? Well . . . There they are.
Are you kidding?!
A pair of baby scissors, a thimble, and a key chain?!! I asked for WEAPONS, Krok!!
Santa Claus is coming . . .

YOU?
ME!
EXPRESS

Listen, Santy Claus, I'm Supermuscleman, the most powerful man in the universe! And I want my presents NOW!
Yeah!

Were you good this year?

Who cares if he was good! We've got money! So shut up, hand over the presents, and get lost!
Yeah!

All right. Follow me.

Merry Christmas.
YIPPEE!
DECAPITATORRR!
VINCE
STAN
DECAPITATORRR!

Look, Krok! I love it!
Don't hurt yourself, Supermuscleman!
Can I light the tree now, Uncle Yellow?
Go ahead.
Z33333
MERRY CHRISTMAS, SUPERMUSCLEMAN AND DOC KROK!!
SLAM!

BANG
ZAP!
RATATATAT!
Ouch!
ZAP!
ZIIIIIP
Eeeeek!
Thanks for the cool fireworks display, Uncle Yellow! MWAH!
Thanks, Captain! MWAH!
HA HA HA! Call me SANTA CLAUS, kids!
The END

Writer: Emmanuel Guibert
Artist: Joann Sfar
The Mix-and-Mingle Suit
SUPERMUSCLEMAN
Want to go, kids?
Ooh, yes, Captain! Let's go!
Town Hall Meeting–TONIGHT!
We promise not to be good!

Meanwhile . . .
Supermuscleman, you have to mix and mingle after your speech tonight.
AGAIN?! I already did, just last week!
I made you a special mix-and-mingle suit. Here, try it on.
I hate to mix and mingle.
What are all these hands for? I look like a centipede!
They'll help you wade through the crowd without getting tired.
Here's the remote control. . . .
You try out your new suit. I have to go write your speech now.
OK, I'll see you later.

Later that night . . .

People of the universe . . .

PRESIDENT

SUPERMUSCLEMAN

ONLY

THE STRONG

SUPER

I want to talk to you ...
I . . . ?
You want to talk to me, Doc Krok?
No, dingbat! You want to talk to them!
OH! I . . . YEAH! I'm the one that wants to talk to them . . . uh, I mean . . . you!
Boy oh boy...
Boy oh boy ...
What a moron!!
This guy is too much!

Tell me, Sir, what do you fin
so great about President Supermuscle-man?
The President? He's the best!
SMM
PRESIDENT SUPERMUSCLEMAN
e's really strong!
And he's so handsome, too!
Don't you think he's pretty stup ..
Look! The President's going to mix and mingle!
SMM
PRESIDENT SUPERMUSCLEMAN
Don't push, Doc Krok!
Don't worry, Super-muscleman. I'm right here with you.

Why's he wearing that strange belt?
Heehee! That gives me an idea, Little Louie. . . . Get your glue gun!
?
See Doc Krok's remote control? . . . Get it for me!
Sweet!
Thanks to your mix-and-mingle suit, Supermuscleman, you can shake hands without actually touching anyone!
You're right, it's very practical.
HEY!
Sploosh!

I got it!
You rock, Little Louie!

Uncle Yellow, take the remote control. I want Supermuscleman to punch as many people as he can!
Got it!

We're going to the podium! Come on, Little Louie!
Can I talk into the microphone?
SUPE

Uh . . . Doc Krok? I don't want to mix and mingle anymore!
AARGH! Someone stole my remote control!

HA HA HA!
Supermuscleman, your approval ratings are going down!

The President just punched me!

Me, too!
He's really strong!!

SMM

SUPERMUSCLEMAN!
Stop your arms!

I don't like this!
I want out!!

SMACK!
SMACK!
SMACK!
SMACK!
Ouch!
Ouch!
SMACK!
SMACK!
SMACK!
SMACK!
Oooph!

Give me the mike!
I get one, too!
HELLO, EVERYONE! This is SARDINE FROM OUTER SPACE talking!
AND LITTLE LOUIE!
ARE YOU TIRED OF GETTING PUNCHED IN THE FACE BY PRESIDENT SUPERMUSCLEMAN?
AND GETTING YOUR EARS BOXED?
?
?
?
?
SARDINE! Wait'll I get my hands on you!
SMACK!
Yeah, I am tired of it!
We clap for him and he beats us up!
It's an outrage!
DOWN WITH SUPER-MUSCLEMAN!
SMM

ANYTIME YOU DECIDE TO GO MIXING AND MINGLING, SUPERMUSCLEMAN, LET SARDINE LEND A HAND!

SMACK!

SMACK!

SMACK!

SMACK!

OUCH!

SMACK!

SMACK!

SMACK!

Ha! Ha!

Ha!

Ha!

Ha!

Ha!

Ha!

Ha!

Ha! Ha!

Ha!

Ha!

HaHa!

Ha!

The End!

Writer: Emmanuel Guibert
Artist: Joann Sfar
103° Fahrenheit
What's wrong with Sardine?
She has a fever, Little Louie. Come on, let's make her a nice cup of tea with honey.

MEANWHILE, ON PLANET BUBULINA ...

Channel 103

103 FM

Tonight is HOT HOTHOT on 103 FM!

AAAH!
Supermuscleman, take off your head-phones!
Wha . . . what was that music?
It's a one-man band! He can hit a pan with a fork, grind his teeth, snort like a pig, and crack his knuckles, all at once.
It's awful. . . .

These are the Channel 103 TV studios, Supermuscleman!

THE TELEVIRUS!

Here we have ridiculous monsters in a hideous set, engaging in absurd and repetitive battles!
Don't you think Sardine might like that?

No way! But, like the radio program, it will fill her thoughts, worry her...
...AND MAKE HER SICK!

Take this space ogre.... Right now, Sardine is dreaming that he's about to eat her...

...And she can't fight back!
RROAAARR

GROOWL!
ARF!

HISSSSSSSS!
Where'd that cat come from?
That's Sardine's cat!

How'd he get in here?
That filthy animal sneaks in everywhere! We've got to catch it!

He's leaving the studio!
CUT! Stop the cameras!!

103 TV apologizes for this temporary break in programming. . . .
Mmm ...

Where'd he go?
He went into the 103 FM offices!!
CURSES! He released the one-man-band!
SKREE!
SNURFFLE!
BLARGH!
CRAACK!
I'll get the cat! You take care of the rest!
What'd you say?
SNIRFL

Here, kitty kitty . . .

Get back to work, all of you! This is a live broadcast!

AAARGH!

BLARGH!

SKREE! SNURFFLE!

SNORT

CRAACK!

Hee hee

ha hee ha

AAAAH!

Here, Sardine, drink this lemon tea!
Lemon tea? How come?

Well...because you have a fever....
Not anymore I don't! I want ice cream!...

...and lots of kitty treats. He really deserves them!
MRRR...

I had the craziest dream. Supermuscleman and Doc Krok were there. . . .
They're the ones who deserve to get sick!
Yum
yum
SLURP
SLURP
Gulp
Scratch
103 fM
We're sunk, Doc Krok!
What? What'd you say?
SNURFFLE!
SKREE!
AAARGH!
Kling
Klang
bubu
CRAACK!
BLARGH!
Bzzzzt
The End

Writer: Emmanuel Guibert
Artist: Joann Sfar
The Yogurt Thieves
Little Louie, are you sleeping?
ASTERPEEKS
the COW BOY
POP
The Schmlurfs
Nrrr . . .
Devil by Night
Devil by Day
DD
H

Did you say NRRR or NO?
YZZZ...
Did you say YZZZ or YES?
NRRR ...
Go ahead and sleep then, you baby! I'm going for a walk!
YZZZ...
It's so annoying that Little Louie is always asleep when I'm not even tired!
Rrrow...
Uncle Yellow, too. He snores so loudly!
SNORRGG
zzz
Peter Pan

You know what, kitty? Since no one wants to play with us, we're gonna have a nice glass of milk.
Myum!
GALLOPING GALAXIES! The fridge is empty!
BOOM! BOOM!
And there's someone in the freezer!
A white lady!
MMMPH ... MMMPH!

Are you the Snow Queen?
I'll explain later. Untie me, quickly!

Where are you taking us?
I'm going after those fridge looters! Buckle up!

WOW!

I didn't know we had a refrigerocket!
It's an old model with a manual defroster. It should really be replaced.

Who are you, anyway?
I'm the Ice Watcher. I'm the one who keeps an eye on your ice cream and space yogurt while you're sleeping.

Not long ago, two guys broke into the fridge. They took me by surprise, tied me up, and stole all your dairy products before escaping.
Ah! What pigs!

We'll get them, though! Their ship must have a leak. It's leaving a trail of milk behind. All we have to do is follow it.
What a waste! With all the little aliens who are starving!

MEANWHILE . . .
Milk, yogurt, cheese, ice cream, pudding . . . We really hit the jackpot this time, Doc Krok!
Hee Hee Hee! Those kids won't get big and strong now, Supermuscleman!
Astrofruit on the Bottom. YUM! I love these!
SLURP
Another milk bottle stolen from the mouth of a babe!
We're approaching the Milky Way. We'll dump our booty here and then go back for more.
TOLL
Have you checked your expiration date?
Now entering THE MILKY WAY
Got fuel?
Welcome to the Milk Turnpike

Supermuscleman is approaching. Raise the gate.
I read you. Raising the gate.
TOLL
The empire of milk is yours, Supermuscleman. These toll booths guarantee you money and power!
Bleeech . . . I think I ate too much condensed milk. . . .
ALERT! ALERT! UNIDENTIFIED VEHICLE! LOWER THE GATE!
Ping! Ping! Ping!
Ping! Ping! Ping!
I read you. Lowering the gate.
TOLL

CRACK!
We break it, we take it!

A refrigerocket is shooting ice cubes at us!

Doc Krok, pull over. . . . I don't feel good. . . .

That's Supermuscleman and Doc Krok's space-bat! Slam into it, Ice Watcher!
That's strange. . . .

They're heading straight into a turn. I don't think they see it!
Doc Krok, I'm gonna be siiiiiiick!
SUPERMUSCLEMAN, LET GO OF THE CONTROLS!

LATER . . .

You like tying people up, HUH?! Well, now it's your turn!!

GRR!

Let's go, Sardine! We'll take a spin around the Milky Way and get rid of all those awful toll booths. No one should have to pay for milk!

Doc Krok, I'm getting freezer burn!
Obviously! That awful Sardine put us in the deep-freeze! If only being full of hot air could get us out of this cold spell!
THE NEXT MORNING . . .
ATCHOO!
ATCHOO!
That's funny the fridge has a cold!
Hey, Sardine, I don't remember buying all these yogurts!
I couldn't sleep last night, so I went yogurt shopping!
The End

Writer: Emmanuel Guibert
Artist: Joann Sfar
Gone Fish-ishing
Pu-pull in the ne-nets, Diastolole! We ca-caught so-something!
OK-K, Systolole!
StarGrazer
HELP!
SOMEONE!

HEY!
Get us out of here!
?!
?
It's ta-talking!
It's mo-moving, too!

OH HO HO! A gu-guy and two ki-kids!
Where are your manners?

We were minding our own business on the deck of our ship and you caught us in your net!
Calm do-down.
It was an accide-dent.

We're fish-ishermen ...
... So of co-course, we fish-ish.
Hee! They talk so funny!
Hee! Hee! Hee!

What do you fish-ish for?
You're so dumb, Sardine!
We fish-ish for st-stars.

Then we se-sell them to the arm-my.
They use them to decorate the sold-diers.
WHAT?!

You're robbing the universe of its beautiful stars in order to decorate your generals?
Well, yeah. It's our jo-job.
They pa-pay us for it.

And who pays you?
President Sup-per . . .
...SUPER-MUSCLE-MAN?
Tha-that's the one!

They're specially trained in combat against little children.

Good work, boys!

GLORY TO YOU, SUPERMUSCLEMAN!

This is Private HARDHAND, a slapping and smacking specialist.
Very good.

Private BOTTOMSUP gives the spankings.
Excellent.

Private DRUMBUST is our ear boxer.
Wonderful.

And Private TANGLETOOTH pulls hair.
Keep up the good work.
The universe needs more soldiers like you.

I am pleased, Krok. Let's decorate these men. Where are the stars?
There are Diastole and Systole with them now.

Hi, boys! Good fishing?
Go-good fish-ishing!
Coo-cool!
Step up to receive your first star, soldiers.

SARDINE!!
Hello-llo!
Hee! Stop it! You're making me laugh too hard!
LITTLE LOUIE!

Let's decorate them in order, starting with the boss!
SMACK!
OUCH!

And the second in command.
OOOPH!
SMACK!

Little children!
ATTACK!
I'll spank the little girl and you pull her hair!
I'll smack the boy and you box his ears!

Come and pick on someone your own size!

Heh! Heh! Heh!
PING PING PING
Ha! Ha! Ha!
Hee! Hee! Hee!
Hey!
Oooph!
Ayayay!
Ouch!

WE BEAT THEM, UNCLE YELLOW! Code Name Whippit is down for the count!
Take that! You still want to box my ears?
BING
OUCH! No! That hurts!!
Where'd Supermuscleman and Doc Krok go?
We sa-saw them.
They went tha-that way.
No need to hurry! We'll catch them on their way out!
There's a tra-trap!

Sardine, was it your idea to hang the net outside the door of the KEEL?
Yeah! Just like Diastole and Systole taught us!
This gi-girl is pretty sma-smart.
She'll go fa-far.
Krok, I'm surrounded by idiots and traitors!
Speak up, Supermuscleman. There's a star in my ear!
The End